Lina's EEG Adventure

By **Danielle Perrotta**

Illustrated by **Tracy J. Nishimoto**

Foreword by Eric B. Geller, MD

A
CURIOUS
CONNECTORS
BOOK

AMARNA
BOOKS & MEDIA
www.amarnabooksandmedia.com

Lina's EEG Adventure

Published by Amarna Books & Media, Maplewood, New Jersey

This publication contains the opinions and ideas of the authors. It is intended to provide helpful and informative material on the subject matter covered. It is sold with the understanding that the authors and publisher are not engaged in rendering professional services in the book. If the reader requires personal assistance or advice, a competent professional should be consulted. The authors and publisher specifically disclaim any responsibility for any liability, loss, or risk, personal or otherwise, which is incurred as a consequence, directly or indirectly, of the use and application of any of the contents of this book. No liability is assumed for damages resulting from the use of information contained within.

ISBN-13: 978-0-9828951-7-7

Book and cover design by Thomas Edward West of Amarna Books and Media

All information graphics credited to the Epilepsy Foundation and the use of the "Stay, Safe, Side" information are used by permission of the Epilepsy Foundation and remain their property.

The Curious Connectors logo design is by Sherry Sutton

Contents

Foreword

Chapter 1—Checkers..1

Chapter 2—Sam 5

Chapter 3—Electric Brain? 7

Chapter 4—What's an EEG?..11

Chapter 5—Spikes 21

Chapter 6—Framily 25

Chapter 7—Are Mummies Cute?..29

Chapter 8—The Zoo..35

Chapter 9—Stay, Safe, Side..41

Chapter 10—"A WEEK?"..49

Chapter 11—The Hospital..55

Chapter 12—Call Button 65

Chapter 13—A Mystery..71

Resources

About the Creators

Acknowledgements

Dedication

This book is dedicated to Belli and KK.
My life is so much better and more interesting
having fun and adventures with you.

CURIOUS CONNECTORS

Curious Connectors was founded upon the belief that we are all curious about the world around us and our inner lives. Curiosity compels us to ask questions, make sense of our experiences and connect the dots on our journey. As an educator, Danielle Perrotta believes in the necessity of raising critical thinkers who are empowered to be inquisitive and creative. The mission of Curious Connectors is to use literature to empower children to critically think about themselves and the world around them, be inquisitive, and creative. By encouraging our children to tell their own stories, they can process their feelings, educate others, and demystify topics that are challenging to talk about.

Foreword

As a parent, I know that nothing is more fearful than finding out something may be wrong with your child. When it comes to seizures and epilepsy, fear is complicated by lack of knowledge. Although seizures can occur in up to 1 in 26 people sometime in their lives and seizures most commonly begin in childhood, many people know little about seizures and their treatment. Because seizures can cause unusual behaviors and movements, they can be frightening and bewildering to observers, leading to unnecessary stigmatization.

The testing and treatment process can be frightening for children and their parents as well. As seizures are basically electrical short circuits in the brain, the most important test is the EEG (electroencephalogram). In the EEG, multiple wires are attached to the scalp to record the brain's activity. Having an EEG for the first time can be hard for a child, especially if it requires hospitalization.

Lina comes to rescue us in this delightful book. She is a bright, curious child who experiences a seizure for the first time when she is with her best friend. The story takes us through her journey of diagnostic testing with EEG with good humor and unflagging spirit.

Lina is a fearless detective who launches into investigating her own case. Her story will help children and their parents prepare for their own EEG testing, and understand seizures and epilepsy better. Reading this story together will also help parents and children open their own dialogue to communicate better about this condition. Lina's experiences will help not just children, but also their parents in understanding better what to expect and how to support their children through it.

Lina and her "framily" are great role models for how to cope with epilepsy. Lina is open with her peers and her teachers about her condition. She is surrounded by supportive friends and family to help her through these experiences. I wish all my patients could share Lina's positive experiences.

So snuggle up with your child and open this book and follow Lina on her EEG Adventure!

—Eric B. Geller, M.D.
Director, Adult Comprehensive Epilepsy Center
Institute of Neurology and Neurosurgery at Saint Barnabas

Lina's EEG Adventure

1
Checkers

Lina enjoyed being with friends and family. She played board games, loved to bake cookies, and enjoyed having friends visit and play. She lived with her mom, dad and baby brother, Nate, who was one year old.

One of their favorite things to do as a family was going to the zoo. Mom, known as Liz to her friends, would pack a lunch for them all. Dad, also called Jake, would make sure to buy tickets for the carousel, train and pony rides. They always had great adventures at the zoo.

Lina's best friend was her neighbor, Sam. Sam lived across the street with Mary, her mom.

Most days, Lina and Sam played outside together, but today was rainy and muggy, so they were playing checkers inside.

Just as Sam was about to jump one of Lina's checkers, Lina had a hard time paying attention. "I don't remember whose turn it is."

"It's my turn," responded Sam. She noticed Lina doing something strange with her eyes. "Lina, you're blinking a lot."

"I am?" Lina asked. "I don't even notice it."

Sam called to Lina's mom, "Why is Lina blinking so much?"

Liz put her hand on Lina's head. "No fever." She looked intently into Lina's eyes.

"Lina, your eyes look fine to me. Sam, call me right away if you notice her blinking again. I'm going to get you guys some cookies."

Lina leaned over to move a piece on the board, "I think I…"

She didn't finish her sentence and tumbled off the chair onto the floor. The checkers went flying everywhere. Lina's whole body was shaking.

"Mom! Liz! Come quickly," Sam shouted. She bent over her friend. "Lina! Lina! Are you okay?"

Liz and Mary rushed into the room. Liz got down on the floor. "She's breathing."

Lina was still shaking. Sam turned to her mom.. "What's happening to my friend?" Sam asked.

2

Liz gently rolled Lina onto her side. Lina stopped shaking. Her mom started calling to her, "Lina, can you hear me?"

Lina said "Yes."

Lina tried to sit up, but her mom said, "It's okay. Just lie here for a bit."

"What just happened to me?" asked Lina.

Sam piped up, "We were playing the game and right in the middle of a sentence, you fell onto the floor. You were shaking. I thought you were joking around!"

Lina said softly, "Sorry I ruined the game."

"Don't worry about the game," said Sam.

"Do you remember what happened before you fell off your chair?" asked Liz.

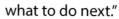

"Nope. I don't even remember falling," replied Lina.

Liz put her arm around Lina. "I'll call Dr. Kravit. I'm sure she will know what to do next."

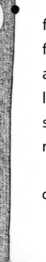

"That was super scary, Lina," said Sam.

Lina yawned and sat further back on the couch, "I feel like I just woke up from a super long nap but I feel like I could go right back to sleep. It's so weird that I don't remember what happened."

"Dr. Kravit said we should come right in," said Liz.

2

Sam

Mary and Sam walked across the street with Nate. Sam sat down on the floor with the baby and Mary started into the kitchen to make a snack.

Sam started to cry. "Don't leave me alone with Nate. What if he falls over and starts to shake?"

Mary put her arms around Sam. "Honey, it must have been really upsetting to see your friend lying there."

Sam wiped her tears. "One minute Lina was fine and then she was on the floor shaking. I was so scared and didn't know what to do."

"I'm sure you were scared," answered Mary. "But you were also calm.

Calling for us was the right thing to do. I'm sure that Liz will call and tell us what's going on with Lina. You can be a good friend by talking with her and helping her."

"How can I help her?" asked Sam.

"I don't know," said Mary. "We have to see what might be wrong first."

Seizure—A seizure happens when there is unusual activity in someone's brain. It can affect the way a person acts or a appears for a short amount of time.

3

Electric Brain?

Dr. Kravit greeted Lina and her mom as she walked into the office. "Can you tell me what happened this afternoon, Lina?"

"I don't remember," said Lina. "I woke up on the floor and felt like I took a long nap. My friend Sam told me I fell off my chair and started shaking."

Liz added, "A couple of minutes before she fell, Sam said that Lina was blinking a lot. I went to get them a snack and then Sam called me because Lina fell."

"That blinking could be a really important piece of the puzzle," said Dr. Kravit. "Your friend Sam is like a detective—she pays attention to details! Let's do a little check-up."

Dr. Kravit asked Lina to stand on one foot, then the other. Next, she asked Lina to push against her hands. The doctor also looked in Lina's eyes and asked Lina if she felt any pain in her head or eyes.

"I don't see anything wrong with you, Lina," Dr. Kravit said. "But I have a strong suspicion that you might have had a seizure."

"What's a seizure?" asked Lina.

Dr. Kravit pointed to a picture of the brain in a poster on the wall. "A seizure happens when there is unusual electrical activity in someone's brain. It can affect the way a person acts or appears for a short amount of time. Your friend Sam saw you fall on the floor and start shaking. Those are some symptoms of a seizure."

Lina turned to the doctor. "Wait. You mean there's electricity in my brain?"

Dr. Kravit began, "Our brains control all of our functions, so there's always a lot of electric activity going on there at any moment. Sometimes there is activity that shouldn't be happening. That can cause a seizure."

Dr. Kravit continued, "There's a special doctor called a neurologist who can do more tests and help us figure out what's going on in your brain." The doctor handed Liz a slip of paper. "Here's her name and number. She will make sure you get the tests you need."

"What should we do if this happens again?" asked Liz.

Dr. Kravit opened a drawer. "Here's a sheet on first aid for seizures. As long as Lina is breathing fine, bring her right back to the office, but you'll need to take her to a hospital on the weekends."

When they walked out, Lina turned to her mom. "I don't want to go to the hospital."

"I know," said Liz, "Let's call the neurologist as soon as we get home."

When they arrived home, Lina's dad was making dinner. "So? What's up, guys?"

"Don't worry, Daddy," said Lina. "We are going to be like detectives and figure it out with the new—what's that word, Mom?"

Liz smiled. "Neurologist. We're seeing her first thing tomorrow."

"I'll take off the morning from work and we will go together. Let's see if Mary can watch Nate again," said Dad.

Neurologist: a doctor who studies the nervous system and specializes in medical issues that affect the brain.

Seizure First Aid

How to help someone having a seizure

1 **STAY** with the person until they are awake and alert after the seizure.
✓ **Time** the seizure   ✓ Remain **calm**
✓ Check for **medical ID**

2 Keep the person **SAFE**.
✓ Move or guide away from **harm**

3 Turn the person onto their **SIDE** if they are not awake and aware.
✓ Keep **airway clear**
✓ **Loosen tight clothes** around neck
✓ Put **something small and soft** under the head

Call 911 if...

► Seizure lasts longer than 5 minutes
► Person does not return to their usual state
► Person is injured, pregnant, or sick
► Repeated seizures
► First time seizure
► Difficulty breathing
► Seizure occurs in water

Do NOT

✗ Do **NOT** restrain.

✗ Do **NOT** put any objects in their mouth.
✓ **Rescue medicines can be given** if prescribed by a health care professional

Learn More and Register for Training: **epilepsy.com/firstaid**

EPILEPSY FOUNDATION
END EPILEPSY TOGETHER

This publication was created by the Epilepsy Foundation, a nationwide network organization. | **National 24/7 Helpline 1.800.332.1000 | epilepsy.com**
This publication is made possible with funding from the Centers for Disease Control and Prevention (CDC) under cooperative grant agreement number 1NU58DP006256-04-00. Its contents are solely the responsibility of the Epilepsy Foundation and do not necessarily represent the views of the CDC. EFA440/PAB0220 Rev. 02/2020 ©2020 Epilepsy Foundation of America, Inc.

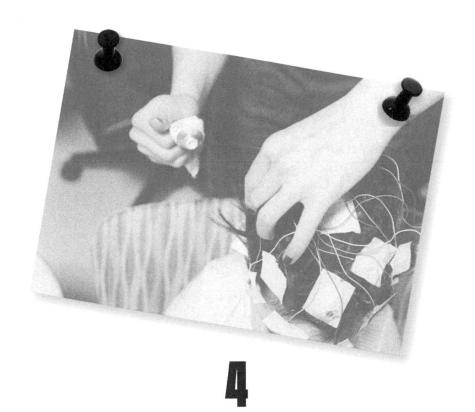

4

What's an EEG?

The next morning, Lina woke up early and got dressed. As her mom prepared breakfast, Lina peppered her with questions. "What kind of doctor am I going to see? What will the doctor do? What will she say is wrong?"

"You sure have lots of questions this morning!" Liz responded. "You can ask Dr. Maleni anything you want. She learned how to take care of people's brains in medical school."

Dad walked in the kitchen holding Nate. "Hey, kiddo! Ready to head to the neurologist's office?"

All of a sudden, Lina looked worried. "I know the doctor is going to do some tests on my brain. But will it hurt?"

"Actually, your mom and I did some detective work last night. There are a lot of different tests they can do. Why don't you ask the doctor if they hurt? In order to solve the big mystery, the doctor has to collect evidence!" said Dad.

"Okay! I'm ready then. Let's go!" shouted Lina.

Dad started packing up Nate's diaper bag, "Well, let's finish eating and get Nate over to Mary and Sam's place. We leave in 10 minutes. Please go brush your teeth."

Across the street, Mary had been talking with Sam over breakfast.

"What can I do to help Lina now?" Sam asked.

"It would be great if you wish her good luck at the doctor's office and ask her about how the test went when she comes home," replied Mary.

When Lina and Jake knocked on the door to drop off Nate, Sam opened the door and hugged her best friend. Her words tumbled out in a rush.

"Hi Lina! My mom told me all about the doctor and the tests and I just want to wish you the very best of luck."

"Thanks, Sam. Dr. Kravit said the eye blinking was a clue to help us figure out what's going on. I got this new notebook to keep track of what the doctor says and to write down clues and evidence."

"Hold on a second," Sam ran to the desk in the living room and came back with washi tape, a blue pen, paper clips, and a little pencil case, "Here! Now you have some supplies for all of the evidence you'll collect and to tape in the pictures you take."

"Thanks, Sam! Okay, so when I get back, let's look at all of the clues and what the tests say. This is like a big mystery. Maybe WE can solve it!" Lina said enthusiastically.

"Yes! That actually sounds like fun—but good luck on the tests… I know you will rock it!" Sam put her hand up and Lina slapped it.

During Lina's first visit to the neurologist, she was very calm and interested in getting to know the doctor. Dr. Maleni asked some of the same questions that Dr. Kravit asked. She also asked lots of questions about her eye-blinking and asked if Lina stared off into space a lot.

"Hmmm, I never noticed it that much, but sometimes I do have to say Lina's name a few times to get her attention," said Jake. "And it's not when she is watching TV or preoccupied—it's when she is sitting and eating dinner or in the back seat while we're driving."

Dr. Maleni turned to Lina. "Lina, did you hit your head recently—at the pool or at the playground? Maybe it wasn't so bad and you forgot to tell your mom and dad?"

"Nope, not that I can remember," said Lina, "I don't run around THAT much outside lately because the weather has been so rainy. Nothing has happened this week for sure."

Lina noticed that Dr. Maleni was taking notes about all they said.

"Why are you writing down everything I say?" asked Lina, "Am I in trouble?"

"I'm writing down information to help me figure out what's going on in your brain. It's not just the tests, but also what you report to me that will help me," replied Dr. Maleni.

"Oh! You're collecting evidence! My friend Sam and I are detectives working on the case!" said Lina, "I guess I should pull out my own notebook and supplies!"

"It is an investigation," said Dr. Maleni with a smile. "Let's gather more evidence." She had Lina walk on a line putting one foot in front of the other and give her a high five with each hand.

"Sometimes we need to do tests with special equipment," the doctor said. "This morning you're going to have a test called an EEG to examine how your brain is working."

"What's an EEG?" asked Lina, poised over her notebook.

Dr. Maleni explained, "EEG is short for electroencephalogram. We'll put electrodes attached to wires all over your head. Those get attached to a computer which will record the electrical activity for about 30 minutes and we can see if you have any activity that is unusual."

"Okay," replied Lina. "Do I have to write anything? At school when I take a test, there is a lot of writing or I have to fill out a bubble sheet."

"You won't be doing any writing, but you do have to follow the instructions our technician gives you. Julie will tell you more as she sets up the test," Dr. Maleni explained.

All of a sudden, Lina looked worried. "But will it hurt?"

"No, but you might get a little itchy. Julie will put the wires on with sticky stuff and tape so they stay on," said Dr. Maleni, "And it's not too much fun if they get tangled in your hair."

Lina and her parents went to another room in the office. The technician greeted them. "Hi, Lina. I'm Julie. Lie down on the bed and I'll put all of these cool wires called "electrodes" on your head and over your heart."

Lina saw a TV and DVD player in the room. "The doctor told me it won't hurt, but if it's going to take a long time, can I watch a video?"

"Sure," replied Julie, "But once we are all set up, you have to stop watching the show, cool?"

Lina laid back on the bed. Julie prepared mixtures at her work station. "What are you doing?" asked Lina.

"Well, first I mix up the paste. It has to be fresh so the electrodes will stick. I also like to cut pieces of tape beforehand so I can work more **quickly.**" Julie held up a red pencil. "Next, I'm going to mark important places on your forehead and temples as a reference point. The marks will help me know where to put the electrodes."

"But HOW do you KNOW where they need to be?"

"You ask important questions, Lina," Julie said.

"I'm a brain detective!" Lina said proudly.

"I'm putting the electrodes over special places, or lobes, of your brain," Julie answered.

"That's cool." said Lina slowly, "Wait, when you do this test will you be able to tell where my seizure came from and if I'm going to have any more?"

"We can only see what your brain is doing right now," Julie answered.

"I can't wait to tell my friend Sam about this. Mom, definitely get some pictures of this!" Lina exclaimed, opening to a fresh page in her notebook where she wrote "TESTS" at the top of the page.

"For sure," Mom replied.

Julie leaned towards Lina and made an "X" mark on her forehead, then two more marks on her temples. Lina wrinkled her nose.

"It doesn't hurt, but it IS weird that you are writing on me!" Lina made a funny face and everyone laughed.

"Just a little warning," explained Julie, "I'm going to rub your scalp with a little bit of alcohol to remove oil from your scalp and make sure the glue sticks. It may smell bad for a few minutes."

Julie used a cotton ball to rub the oil off her head and Lina squirmed in her chair. "How many wires are going on my head?"

"There are about 20 wires altogether. The computer screen on the wall shows the wires as they are hooked up. Right now they are all red. But when I connect them to the recorder and run the test to make sure they are on correctly, we will see them turn green,"

"How do you know which wire is which if there are so many?" inquired Lina. "Can you tell by the colors?"

"Each wire is a different color, but that's not how I tell. I plug each wire into this recorder you'll carry around. Each hole is labeled with a different number or letter combination and those numbers and letters are also on the screen."

Julie continued to glue electrodes on Lina's head. Lina was fascinated by the process, "It's like you are doing a dance!"

"What do you mean, Lina?" her dad asked.

"Well, there's a rhythm to it. First, she puts on the alcohol, then she puts down the glue, she presses the electrode in and puts the tape on top. There's a pattern and I feel it the same way every time on my scalp." She clapped her hands rhythmically, "Alcohol, glue, electrode, tape."

"We know this is going to provide more evidence to figure out the great Lina mystery," interjected dad.

While Julie checked all of the electrode connections, Lina wrote the EEG steps in her notebook.

"Good news," Julie said, "You are all hooked up and we can start the test now."

"During the test, I'm going to present you with a lot of lights, pinwheels, silly toys. The room will be dark except for this light," Julie pointed to a small light at the top of her desk, "And for part of it, I'll turn this off and just have a flashing light on."

"Why do you need to flash lights in my eyes?" asked Lina.

"Well, the lights make your brain react by adjusting to the lights or maybe doing something it's not supposed to do," Julie started, "And then…"

"Wait! Why do you want my brain to do something wrong—isn't it supposed to be getting fixed?"

Mom reached out for Lina's hand and held it tight, "Honey, the test has to try and figure out what might have made your brain act funny."

"If you should have a seizure or your eyes start blinking, we can record that with the machine," Julie added.

"Now it doesn't seem very adventurous. It feels a bit scary," Lina admitted.

"That's totally natural. The test is only 20 minutes. That's shorter than it took to put on the electrodes!" Julie explained, "When it's all done we can talk about how it felt, but during the test, you need to be quiet."

"Okay," Lina said, "Let's do this!"

"You've got this," whispered Mom and Dad as they kissed Lina's cheeks.

Twenty minutes went by with Lina taking in everything that Julie did. First, she shone a light in her eyes. Then she made the light blink like when everyone was dancing at Lina's cousin's wedding—but no music was on. She was told to blow on a pinwheel so the pinwheel spun around just like the one in her yard at home.

The last thing Julie did was show Lina some toys and ask her to follow the toy with her eyes as Julie moved it around and around in different positions.

"All done," Julie proclaimed. "I'll share this with the doctor and when you come in later this week, she will review the results with you."

"Not today?" Lina inquired, disappointed. "I just want to know what's going on with my brain right now."

"Dr. Maleni has to look at the EEG and determine what is happening. She needs to take some time to figure it out and make a plan that she can share with you and your family."

"I guess she has to analyze the "evidence" before she comes to any conclusions, like a good detective," said Lina.

"Okay, now I'm going to start taking off the electrodes," said Julie.

"Ouch!" cried out Lina. "Stop—it hurts!"

"Sorry, Lina. Your hair got a little stuck in the glue. I'm trying really hard to take the electrodes out carefully," Julie said, "Let me use some water. That will make it come off a little easier."

"It's GUNK—and I'm definitely taking a bath to get it all out," said Lina.

5

Spikes

Lina and her mom went to Mary and Sam's house to pick up Nate. Sam greeted them at the door. "Mom! They're back!" and she hugged Lina.

Nate toddled over to Lina for a hug too. She kissed him and played a couple of rounds of peek-a-boo.

"How did it go?" asked Sam, "Did the doctor figure out what happened? Is there anything wrong with your brain?"

"I don't know yet," answered Lina, "The EEG test was really weird. The doctor will tell us Thursday what's going on."

"Sure," replied Sam. "Want some lunch? My mom made us pasta

salad and there are some apples on the counter."

"Yeah, I'm actually really hungry," grinned Lina. "My mom took a bunch of pictures so we could show you. Check out my crazy hair!" Lina lifted her baseball cap and make a funny face.

"Ewwww! Gunk!" Sam laughed.

"That's what I called it," Lina giggled.

Thursday arrived faster than any Thursday Lina could remember. Between summer camp every day, trips to the pool, and play dates with Sam, she was always busy.

Mom and Dad went to the appointment with Lina.

"Can we see the EEG?" Lina asked. "I want to see what my brain is doing!"

Dr. Maleni opened a manila folder and took out pages with tons of scribbles. "Where is the EEG?" Lina asked.

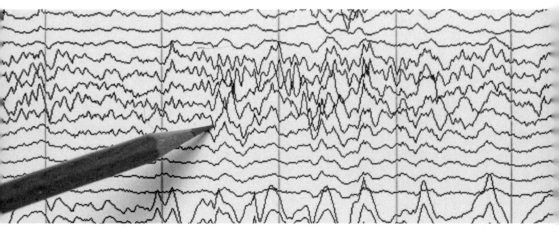

"This is it," said Dr. Maleni, "I know these look like scribbles, but those are your brainwaves. Lina, the EEG didn't show any seizures, but it recorded these unusual spikes." She took out a highlighter from her breast pocket on her lab coat and outlined a small portion of the lines. "This a spike right here and another one here."

Lina saw her parents exchange concerned looks. "What does that mean, spikes?" she asked.

"Spikes show abnormal brain activity. We don't know if you are having seizures, but we don't know if you aren't either."

"Wait! Let me understand this, Lina might have been having seizures for a while? And you think she still might be having seizures?" Jake asked, "How come we didn't notice it?"

Dr. Maleni addressed them all. "Well, Sam noticed the rapid blinking. Not all seizures show up by someone falling down or shaking. Some seizures just involve staring spells or brief moments of blanking out without anyone noticing—even the person having the seizure. I'm going to order some more tests and we are going to figure out if you have epilepsy."

"What's epilepsy?" asked Lina.

"Epilepsy is a brain disorder. That means there is electrical activity in a brain that is not supposed to be happening," Dr. Maleni stated. "Some people have epilepsy because someone in their family had it and it's passed on to other family members." As Dr. Maleni talked she pointed to colorful graphs on the wall. "Other people get it from head injuries or accidents. Some other people get it and we don't know why."

"Lina's dad rubbed her head and smiled. "Dr. Maleni, what's our next step?"

"Well, we can start Lina on two pills of this medication." She wrote down the information on a prescription pad.

"Does the medicine come in bubble gum flavor like my cough syrup?" asked Lina.

Spikes—On an EEG reading, the spikes are an indication of abnormal brain activity; sometimes they indicate the start of a seizure.

"Unfortunately, it's a capsule that your parents will open and sprinkle on to different foods you like, so no bubble gum flavor," said Dr. Maleni.

"Are there any side effects?" asked Mom.

"Well, we will need to do blood tests every now and then to make sure that it's not hurting Lina's liver. There are some other side effects, but you should read the insert that comes with the bottle for the full list."

"Then you can come back in two weeks for an ambulatory EEG to see if it's controlling the seizures or if you need to take more medication. Do you have any questions?"

"Wait! What? Blood tests? Ambulatory EEG? Does that mean in an ambulance?" Lina asked, alarmed.

"The ambulatory EEG is like the one in the office, but we send you home with a recorder for two days. As far as the blood test goes, sometimes people who are taking these medications have problems with their liver that can be serious." Dr. Maleni said gently. "We're looking for clues, Lina."

"Thanks, doc," replied Lina. "Nice to have you on this case!"

6

Framily

They were all a little quiet walking out of the building. Lina looked pensive and Jake held her hand.

Lina broke the silence, "Okay. So now we kind of know what's wrong and I can take medicine."

"Yes," said her mom slowly, "But Daddy and I need to read more about spikes and learn about how to help you. Knowing more information will help all of us."

"Well, I want to show Sam the EEG and I want to read the information, too," Lina said. "This is my body and my brain and this is happening to me so I want to know what's up."

"Okay," said Dad. "Taking medication is new to you so we are going to check in with you on how you are feeling. Why don't we make a log to record any side effects too?"

Lina sighed but said, "Okay. Let's do it."

When they arrived home, Mary and Sam were playing with Nate in the living room. "Hey, kiddo!" Mary said, "How did the appointment go?"

"The EEG didn't show that I had a seizure in the office," said Lina. "It shows that I have spikes that can turn into seizures. Now I am going to start taking medication."

"Dr. Maleni said that some people have seizures and don't even know it," Lina said emphatically, "Maybe that's what was happening when I was blinking!"

"Whoa!" Exclaimed Sam. "That's…whoa. I want to say it's cool, but not 'cool, good,' just sort of amazing that your brain is doing something that you don't know about. Is that why you fell on the floor?"

"Maybe. Here is my EEG readout," Lina pulled out the folder from her mom's bag, "See here, where the highlighter is, that's a spike. In. My. Brain."

"We all have to watch for the blinking and keep an eye on Lina, but, hopefully, the medication will help," added Liz.

"The doctor also gave me some websites to look at and there are videos we watch that will tell us more information about EEGs," said Lina.

"I want to check out the websites too," said Sam.

"Great," said Lina, "Especially because I'm going to have another EEG like the one I had a couple of weeks ago but at home. And I'm going to do all the stuff I usually do, like go to the park, go to the zoo, and go shopping. I can travel anywhere with the EEG machine as long as I don't get wet."

Jake spoke up, "Lina's neurologist will be able to see how Lina's brain is working while on the medication and while she is doing things that we can't do in the doctor's office, like sleeping, playing with her brother, or watching a movie."

"And having a playdate with me!" Sam added. Suddenly Sam's brow furrowed. "Wait, it's the end of the summer. That means you'll be in school for the EEG. What do you think kids will say?"

"We can put all of the research we do into a presentation to teach kids about EEGs. And I can be the example of a person who has it!" Lina said excitedly.

"Group hug!" commanded Sam. The girls hugged and Nate crawled in between their legs, making them all laugh.

"Okay—we are a framily with a plan," said Lina.

"What's a framily?" asked Sam.

"Family + friend—your friends are so close they are like family!" Lina said excitedly.

Sam high-fived Lina. "To framily!"

"The best framily!" Lina high-fived her back.

My EEG

7

Are Mummies Cute?

Lina and Sam spent the last week of the summer researching EEGs and seizures between trips to buy school supplies, new clothes and having framily BBQs, ice cream on summer nights and swimming in the local pool.

The letters from their new teacher arrived the next week. Lina and Sam were excited to find out they had the same teacher, Mr. Delion. Phone calls and play dates revealed that they knew almost everyone in their class.

The first week of school was a whirlwind, getting to know their teacher and playing lots of icebreaker games to get to know each other.

At the end of the week, Lina and Sam lingered after school to talk to Mr. Delion.

"We were hoping to ask you about something. Do you have a minute?" asked Lina.

"Sure," said Mr. Delion looking at the girls. "What can I do for you?"

"Well, I had an adventurous summer. I had to start seeing a neurologist." Lina looked at Mr. Delion's concerned face.

"It's been an adventure because we think Lina had a seizure and we have been researching all about EEGs and using clues from her tests to figure out what's going on," Sam interjected.

Mr. Delion said, "Your mom and the nurse already talked to me so I would know what to do if you have a seizure in class."

"Oh, I know," said Lina. "But Sam and I were hoping we can do a presentation to the kids in class. I have to have an EEG test starting next Monday after school so I want to let the kids know at morning meeting on Monday and then do a short presentation with Sam on Tuesday. Would that be okay?"

"That's a great idea, Lina. I think the kids will learn a lot."

"Thanks, Mr. Delion!"

Over the weekend, the girls gathered all of their information and made a slideshow.

On Monday, Lina and Sam sat in morning meeting. "Are you nervous?" Sam asked.

"I wasn't until you asked," Lina laughed.

Soon it was Lina's turn to share her goals for the week. "I'm pretty excited for this week's goal. Today I'm going to the doctor to start taking a test. It's called an electroencephalogram or EEG for short. It's a test to record my brainwaves. One big thing you should know is that I'll come in tomorrow morning looking like a mummy." The kids giggled. Lina continued, "Well, not exactly, but my head will be wrapped in gauze and I'll be wearing this little backpack holding the EEG recorder. You'll see. This is going to be a great adventurous week!"

Lina looked at Sam and exchanged a smile. Sam gave her a thumbs up and mouthed "Good Job!"

That afternoon at Dr. Maleni's office, Julie attached the electrodes on Lina's head again.

"What if a wire comes loose at my house? Can we plug it into our computer at home to check it?"

"I'm afraid not, but that's a super cool idea. Maybe someday some smart kid like you will develop an app for that," said Julie, "Meanwhile, as long as the screen on this little device is on, you should be fine."

The EEG recorder was about the size of Lina's video game player at home. "This screen shows the time and how long the machine has been recording. It also has a button. Mom and Dad need to press the button if anything unusual happens. You also have a big job of pressing the button when you wake up in the middle of the night. It could be something in your brain that is waking you up."

"What would be unusual?" asked Liz.

"If Lina has a seizure, you would press the button. But if you notice her staring into space for a long time or blinking rapidly, that's a good time to press the button too. When Dr.

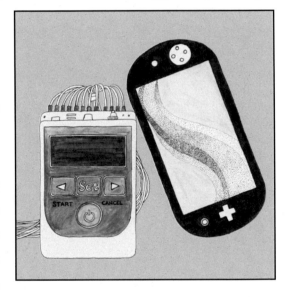

Maleni looks at your EEG, she can tell if you were having a seizure when you pressed the button," Julie explained. "Here is a log and instructions. The biggest rules are on the first page. Every time you press the button, write down what Lina was doing."

"No gum chewing, no showers or baths, no sweating," said Lina. "Well, it's still pretty hot in September. Not sure how the whole 'no sweating' thing is going to work, but I can do the others!"

Lina cried, "Ooooh, I don't like to say this, but I hope that something happens if it helps you figure out more about my brain."

Julie put the EEG machine in a little backpack that Lina would wear all day and sleep with at night.

"Mom, get some pictures of me for my school presentation," said Lina.

When they got in the car, Lina caught a glimpse of herself in the rearview mirror, "Whoa! I really do look like a mummy!" She exclaimed.

"A cute mummy!" Her mom responded.

"I hope people are cool about it. I don't want to have to deal with people making fun of me."

"Why do you think people might make fun of you?" her mom asked.

"Well, when something is different, people notice and then point it out in a not-so-nice-way," Lina started, "Having an EEG makes me different, but that isn't a bad thing. I just have to teach people about it so it doesn't seem strange."

"I think you're doing something that's going to make a difference," Mom said.

"I hope it won't be something people ever make fun of or are afraid of," added Lina.

8

The Zoo

"Hey guys, I'm hoooooome," Lina called as she knocked on Sam's screen door.

"I'll be right.." Sam stopped and looked at Lina through the screen. "Whoa!"

Lina turned red. "Uh oh, does it look terrible?"

Sam responded quickly, "No, uh, just different! Does it itch?" She wrinkled her nose and opened the door. "Once people get used to it, it will be no big deal," said Sam reassuringly.

"Maybe I should wear a hat at first," said Lina thoughtfully.

"Hmmm, I have a witch's hat," said Sam.

"Uh, won't that just call attention to me more?" asked Lina.

Sam ran back with a black Halloween witch's hat. "Yeah, but then they will be so surprised about the hat that they will be less surprised about the bandage thingy."

"Maybe we should leave off the hat. But, maybe I need to test out being around lots of people! Hey mom, can we go to the zoo?" Sam asked, "And then we can take some great pictures to show the kids how I can go anywhere with the EEG recorder AND my head wrapped like this!"

"Super idea," said Sam.

Lina's mom looked at Mary, "I guess we are going to the zoo!"

As soon as they dashed through the gates of the zoo, Lina turned to Sam. "What should we do first? Monkeys? Train? Sea lion? Or," she giggled, "See THE lion? Ha ha!"

"I want to take the train!" exclaimed Sam.

"Cool. Let's do it," replied Lina.

A little boy pointed to Lina's head while waiting on line for the train and asked, "What happened to your head? Did you have an accident?"

"No accident. My friend Sam and I are detectives trying to solve a mystery! I'm having a test done on my brain–it's called an EEG. See, I have this cool backpack with a kind of recorder in it. The doctor is going to tell me what's happening in my brain."

"Cool!" the boy said. "Do you think the doctor would give me one, too?"

"No, it's only if you might have something wrong with your brain," Sam said.

The day continued that way. Lina and her mom recorded their zoo trip in the log that Julie gave to them. Lina didn't have any seizures, but Sam noticed her eyes blinking a couple of times and Lina pressed the button on her machine. Sam wrote down the time, noted that they were watching the monkeys and that Lina's eyes were blinking very fast.

Many people asked questions and some people pointed. When Lina saw someone point, she started shouting, "It's okay, it's an EEG adventure!"

MY SEIZURE EVENT DIARY

NAME: _____

During Seizures		Date/Time	Date/Time	Date/Time	Date/Time	Date/Time	Date/Time	Date/Time
Awareness	Fully Aware							
	Confused							
	Responds to Voice							
	Not Responsive							
Facial Expressions	Staring							
	Twitching							
	Eyes Rolling							
	Eyes Blinking							
Head Movements	Sudden Head Drop							
	Turns to 1-Side							
	Turns Side to Side							
Body Stiffens	Whole Body							
	Legs							
	Arms							
Jerking Movement	Whole Body							
	Legs							
	Arms							
Automatic Movement	Hands Clapping, Rubbing							
	Lip Smacking, Chewing							
	Walking, Wandering							
	Running							
Speech	Able to Talk Normally							
	Unable to Talk							
	Inchoherent/Nonsense Words							
	Mixing up Words							
Fall	Fall - Yes/No							
After Seizure	Fully Aware							
	Responds Normally							
	Confused							
	Tired							
	Asleep							
	Agitated, Irritable							
	Incontient - Yes/No							
	Injury - Type/No							
Time	Length of Seizure							
	Length of Recovery Period							
Interventions	Rescue Medicine Given							
	VNS Magnet							
Triggers - List any possible triggers								
Name of Observer								

Used with permission from the Epilepsy Foundation of America, Inc., © 2020.

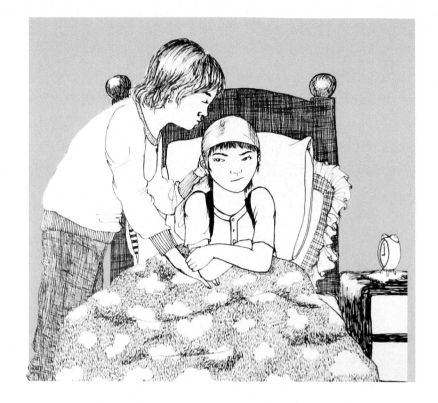

9

Stay, Safe, Side

Back at home, Lina was trying to scratch her scalp under the wrapping with a pencil. "I'm super excited to go to school tomorrow and tell everyone about it. Mr. Delion said I can share during morning meeting," Lina yawned. "Sam's going to help me too. We have a poster and everything."

"Time for bed now, though," Liz said, "Are you comfortable? It must be a little odd to sleep with a backpack."

Lina tried to settle into her bed and moaned, "Oh, man, how am I going to get to sleep tonight?"

"Uh, well, here, let me..." Liz struggled to move the wires around and place the backpack away from Lina's pillow.

"Mom!!! It's pulling my hair when you do that! And what if I wake up in the middle of the night and forget that I have it and I go to the bathroom and it falls? I better wear it."

"I hadn't thought of the whole bathroom thing. Definitely wake me up if you have to go and need help."

"Okay, um, I'm going to try and sleep on this side," said Lina.

"Let me prop you up with the pillows to keep you from rolling over on the backpack," said Mom.

"That's better. Wish me luck!" laughed Lina.

On Tuesday morning, Lina woke up and looked at the clock. She wrote down the time in her log and checked the display screen on the machine. There was nothing on the screen.

"Mom!" Lina called as she walked out of her room into the hallway. "The screen is blank!"

Mom shuffled out of her room rubbing her eyes and Dad followed. "Let's call the doctor," said Dad. "I can drive you to her office before I drop you at school this morning."

"I don't want to miss the presentation, dad!" Lina was upset, "I have to do it during morning meeting."

"I'll let your teacher and Sam know so they can wait for you. These things can't be helped."

When they arrived at the doctor's office, Julie ushered them into an exam room. "The machine must have stopped working in the middle of the night," Lina told her.

"No problem," Julie reassured her. "I'll reset the machine and wrap it in a towel to give it some more protection. Maybe you bumped it in the night or right before you went to sleep. You just have to keep it 48 hours starting over again. That means you will have it for two more mornings."

"So I have to have it all day today and sleep with it for two MORE nights? REALLY?" She made a face and rubbed her neck, "I'm already so sleepy from being uncomfortable last night."

"It's a bummer for sure, kiddo," Dad said, "But maybe we can try a different position tonight. It'll be okay."

"If you say so." Lina did not look convinced.

When Lina walked into class her friends waved hello, then stopped. Some had the same reaction Sam did—a little shock on their face. Lina wished she could have started the day on the blacktop and had a little time to prepare instead of seeing half of her classmates stare at her.

"All right, friends," Mr. Delion stated, "Lina would like to say a couple of words before we get on with the day. Everyone come on over to the rug."

"Hi guys," said Lina awkwardly. "Well, here it is in person...my EEG.

Sam, can you come up here?"

Lina swallowed and looked at her friend gratefully. "Hey Guys," Lina started, "Sam and I are in the middle of a great big mystery."

Sam pulled up the slideshow on Mr. Delion's computer and made it appear on the whiteboard. "Lina is getting an EEG test because she had a seizure two weeks ago when we were having a playdate. And that is where the mystery began."

Some of their classmates gasped. "Oh my gosh," Savion blurted out. "Did it hurt?"

"I didn't even know what had happened after it was over, but Sam was with me the whole time. And because she pays close attention to details, she saw that I was blinking a lot right before it happened and that's a clue that the doctor used."

"My mom took some pictures of me getting the electrodes put on so you guys can see what's under this bandage," Lina said.

"Do the wires zap your brain or anything?" inquired Luisa.

"Nope!" said Lina, "Although, my head gets a little itchy. It IS a bit annoying to sleep with a backpack on...could you imagine?" Everyone laughed.

"Have you had another seizure where you have fallen down?" asked Nasir.

"No, and I hope I don't, but if I do, Sam is going to share some key things you all could do if it happens when we are hanging out in class, at lunch or even if we have a playdate," Lina said.

"Are you still allowed to go on playdates?" Samantha asked.

"Sure!" Sam exclaimed, "She's still Lina. We just have to know what to do."

"Well, what if we catch seizures while we are hanging out with you?" asked Samantha.

"You can't catch seizures, but lots of people have seizures," Lina said.

Stay, Safe, Side

STAY with the person and start timing the seizure.

Keep the person SAFE.

Turn the person onto their SIDE if they are not awake and aware.

"We made this poster for the classroom so we can all remember," said Sam. "We hope that Lina doesn't have a seizure in school, but in case she or anyone you know does, here is a simple phrase to show us what to do: "

"These are the basics and can be super helpful."

"So this is something different about me. You can ask me more at recess or lunch. I am okay talking about it."

"Thank you for sharing with us," Mr. Delion came to the front of the room, "I certainly learned a lot too today. I haven't even met someone with an EEG on their head while in school or ever. I'll put your poster up next to the sink so we can all see it. "

Lina and Sam fielded more questions during lunch and recess, but the day continued pretty normally.

After school, Lina was really excited to talk about the EEG machine. She told the cashiers at the grocery store, her neighbors, and her babysitter after school when they made slime! That night, she and her parents made a more comfy pillow setup to help her sleep better.

The next two days passed with the machine remaining on. Lina was really happy, though, when Thursday morning arrived and the electrodes could come off at home.

Lina sat on a chair they set up in the bathroom. Her mom filled the sink with soapy water. Liz started gently peeling off the tape and electrodes and scrubbing the glue from Lina's scalp.

"Mom," Lina looked at her mom and grabbed her arm, "Am I going to have to do this ever again?"

Her mom took a deep breath and put her arm around Lina's shoulder for a squeeze. "Yes. Every couple of months you may need to have an EEG in the office or at home."

"Oh," Lina's eyes were wide with surprise. "I guess I hadn't really thought about the future that much. I've been just thinking about the day-to-day stuff. I thought that once we got this longer report that we'd be done. You know, mystery solved."

"Until we know what's up, we still need to gather more clues."

"Okay, since that's the case, let's get started taking these off," sighed Lina. "I want to help. That way maybe I can figure out how to make it hurt less."

"Good idea," mom said.

10

"A WEEK?"

A week later, it was time to go to the doctor for the results of the ambulatory EEG. Dr. Maleni walked in the office, greeting them with a smile. "Hi, Lina. How are you today?"

"Nervous," blurted out Lina. "I just want to know what the EEG says."

"Let's take a look," Dr. Maleni responded. She turned to her computer and pulled up Lina's EEG.

"This section shows some spikes that are occurring. Spikes show us that the potential to have a seizure is there, but the good news is that the medication already seems to be controlling the seizures."

"What about when I pressed the button?" Jake asked. "Lina was blinking a lot while watching TV. Was that a seizure?"

"No," replied Dr. Maleni, "none of the times you pressed the button connected with any seizures."

"What about the times I pressed it overnight?" asked Lina.

The doctor paused and looked thoughtful, "I noticed that and I'm glad you brought it up. Okay, let's collect some more clues. You will keep a sleep log for a week—write down the time you go to sleep, naps, and if you wake up in the middle of the night, either write down the time yourself or get your parents to do it. Can you do that?"

"Sure. I have a clock next to my bed," answered Lina.

"I'm going to schedule a hospital video EEG a month from now.

People can have seizures in the middle of the night that don't show up on an EEG at home. But at the hospital, we will be video recording your movements so we can see you as well as have the EEG on your head. We will gather more evidence this way," Dr. Maleni explained.

Liz asked, "How long will that take?"

Dr. Maleni said, "We count on at least 48 hours, but I always tell patients to plan on a week."

"A WEEK??? School just started!" Lina shrieked, "I can't be off for a week."

"We can start on a Friday, so if you don't have to be there for a week, you can be back at school on Monday," said Dr. Maleni.

"What about my friends? There is always so much fun stuff on the weekend," Lina said, sadly.

"Your friends can visit you in the hospital, Lina," Dr. Maleni said gently, "And believe it or not, our hospital does so much to help kids have fun. You can borrow DVDs to watch while sitting in bed, you get breaks during the day to go to the playroom for crafts, and sometimes therapy dogs visit the ward. Even clowns can come through!"

Lina brightened visibly, "Okay, that doesn't sound TOO, TOO bad. As long as the clowns aren't the scary kind. Can my parents come?"

Dr. Maleni smiled, "Absolutely! Mom and dad, gear up for a sleepover!"

"Okay, we have a plan. Now, what about the medicine?" Mom asked.

"It's something that we need to continue to monitor. Lina, you need to have blood tests every three months and EEGs as well in our office or at home," Dr. Maleni said.

Lina smiled weakly, "Okay. I'm not psyched about all these blood tests. I'm going to feel like a pin cushion! Maybe I need to do another presentation about medication and blood tests for the kids at school

to explain why I'll be wearing so many band-aids and why..."

Her dad interrupted, "We can do blood tests before school and we can do some of the EEGs over the weekends. Lina, this doesn't have to take over your life."

"But it already has, Dad," Lina insisted. "My whole life has changed and yes, I can do this stuff out of school, but having this mystery going on is something I'm dealing with every day and people can't see it. If I'm going to go through this and trying to figure it out, I think I should be teaching kids about it so they get it. Maybe people will be more understanding."

"That's a great attitude, Lina," Dr. Maleni said, "But don't put so much pressure on yourself to teach the world. You need to be getting sleep and taking care of yourself."

"But I HAVE to talk about this and we have to figure out what's going on," Lina looked determined.

Dr. Maleni beamed at her, "Remember to lean on your family and friends when you need to."

Sam was waiting for Lina's report. Lina didn't exactly look excited. "What's up? Is everything okay?"

Lina explained what the doctor said and ended with, "I haven't ever been to the hospital and I'm not too worried, but I don't want to miss stuff because I have something wrong with me."

"I'm totally going to come and visit you," Sam said.

"Cool, and we have more information! Dr. Maleni gave us the last EEG printout. And now I have a sleep log to fill out. I have been waking up every night so I have to 'document' it." Lina brightened up. "More mysteries with my sleep!"

She continued, "Good news is that I'm going to have a sleepover with my mom and dad on different nights."

"I can sleep over, too!" Sam said.

"Family only, Sam," Jake said, "but it's

really cool that you want to come. What if you bring Lina to the hospital with us?"

"Okay. That will be fun," Sam said.

"Yeah—it will be cool to have you there. I will miss Nate, though—let's go back in and give him some tickles!" Lina said.

"Ina! Ina! Ina!" Nate cried when she walked in the door.

Lina helped keep her sleep log. She told her parents when she had a hard time falling asleep and whenever she woke up, she wrote down the time. After a week, her mom switched alarm clocks with her and gave her a sleep machine that had soothing sounds like ocean waves and crickets chirping. The second week she had a better time falling asleep but was still waking up in the middle of the night.

11

The Hospital

The afternoon to go to the hospital arrived. Lina grabbed her luggage and Sam helped her load it into the car. Sam tossed in an extra bag of games and puzzles that she thought Lina would like.

Lina was grateful that Sam came along to help her get settled. Lina kissed Nate's face 100 times and told him that she would miss him. His face turned serious and she tickled him, "It's okay, little man! I'll be back before you know it."

He giggled happily, "Ina! Ina! Ove oo!" That was Nate's way of saying "Love you" and Lina loved when he did that.

Mom drove, Dad played DJ and Lina said, "I hope we can play music in the room... REALLY LOUD!"

"There are little kids that have an early bedtime," Mom said.

"Wait, there will be other kids there?" Lina said, "Ha ha! I don't know why I didn't realize that before."

"You can't be super social," Mom said, "You have to spend a lot of time in the bed so they can take that video of you. And the other kids will be getting EEGs too."

"Wow," breathed Sam, "I didn't realize that there is a whole place just for EEGs."

Liz and Jake checked Lina into the hospital and they all rode the elevator up to a colorful waiting room. A security guard called for a nurse to guide them to Lina's room. Sam wrote notes in her notebook.

"Okay, so far, I wrote down the timeline of events, just like we learned on that spy show the other day," Sam said.

"Good. And my dad is taking pics of everything so we can add to our evidence," Lina responded.

The hallway was decorated with colorful animal murals. There were lots of people walking from room to room and pushing carts with equipment down the hallways.

The room had a big hospital bed, a chair to the side, whiteboards on the walls with tic tac toe and puzzles, and a TV mounted to the ceiling. To the left of the bed was a video monitor on the wall.

"I think that might be my bed," Mom pointed to the chair, "Glad I brought a comfy blanket and my pillow!"

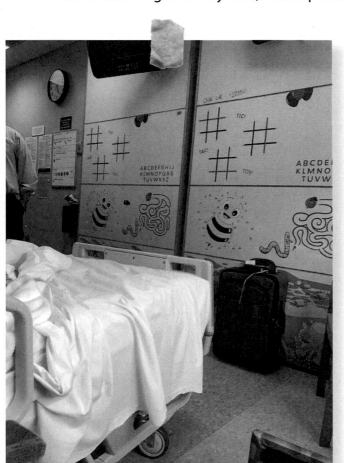

"I can sleep in the chair, Mom," Lina said.

"Nope! You get the cool bed that moves up and down because the video will be on you the whole time."

A tall lady in lime green scrubs with cartoon characters on them had entered the room with a friendly smile. "Hi! I'm Jeannine and I will be your nurse today until 7 pm." Jeannine looked at Sam and Lina. "One of you two ladies must be Lina."

"I'm Lina! This is my best friend Sam, she came to take some notes about my stay here—we are solving a super important mystery!" Lina said excitedly, "I just loooove your scrubs! That show is my favorite!"

"Thanks! Mine too!" Jeannine wrote her name in the whiteboard and said, "We are going to do your EEG test right in this room but I also have to do some other tests too. I need to take some blood in the morning before you take your medication and we will also do a urine test"

"A urine test? What's that?" Sam interjected.

"Lina needs to pee in a cup," Jeannine explained.

The girls laughed. "Wait! How will I do that???" Lina gasped between giggles. She looked at Sam and crossed her eyes.

"We'll figure it out," Mom said.

"If you need a nurse, this remote will be the way that you can contact me or any nurse who is working while you're here. The EEG technician will get you hooked up ASAP so we can get this show on the road. In the meantime, let's order your dinner and your breakfast for tomorrow."

"Let's order pizza!" Lina said, "Like we usually do on Friday nights."

"Here's the menu—usually the hospital has a pretty good selection!" Said Jeannine.

"Yeah, let's take a look. Ooh, they have pudding and mac and cheese. Definitely good for tomorrow," Lina said.

"I packed some cookies, fruit and cut-up veggies so we would have snacks. They don't have 24-hour room service and I figured we might get hungry," Jake replied.

"Let's check these bags out, Sam," said Lina. "Ooh, checkers... uh, let's save that for later. Want to do a puzzle?"

Lina climbed up on the bed and sat on the remote. The bed moved up a little bit. "Oops! I guess I shouldn't sit on this!" Lina played with the buttons and the bed moved. "Hey Sam, come up! Let's go for a ride on the bed."

The girls giggled as the bed went up and down, forward and back. "This is so cool, Lina! I wish I had a bed like this at home!"

"Yeah, I know, me too! Okay, I'm done! Let's use this little table and set up the puzzle," Lina said.

A man walked in the room, "Oh, a puzzle? I love puzzles! I'm Eric, your friendly EEG tech."

"Lina, have you ever had an EEG before?"

"She's kind of a professional," said Sam. Everyone laughed. "Well, she is!"

"Great, the whole EEG process is exactly the same as in the office and at home, except for two things. One, you'll be on camera the whole time," pointing to the camera in the ceiling that Lina didn't see before, "And this video monitor will be on the whole time showing both the EEG and the video of you."

"So cool," Lina breathed.

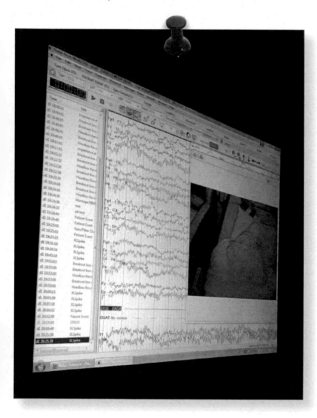

Sam jumped off the bed, "I want to sit over here so I can take pictures and get a good look. This is my first time seeing this and the pictures might come in handy." As Eric started putting the electrodes on Lina's head, Sam and Lina peppered him with questions about the "gunk", the wires, and where he was placing them on Lina's head.

Sam photographed the entire process, trying to get different angles. At some points, Lina started making silly faces and they erupted in giggles.

"All done!" Eric exclaimed, "Mom, since you are staying, you can press this button if you see anything that could be a seizure. And if Lina experiences a seizure where she shakes, there will be technicians monitoring the video, so nurses will be called to come in. If you are awake

and something like that happens, call the nurses, too. If Lina wakes in the middle of the night, press the button. It could be a seizure that's waking her up."

Lina looked at Sam, who was furiously writing in her notebook. "Got all that?"

"If you have to go to the bathroom or want to go to the playroom," Eric continued, "put your backpack on just like you did at home. This cable is plugged into the wall. You can unplug it from the recorder and take the recorder with you. Otherwise, leave the recorder on the stand next to your bed. If you leave and come back, you have to remember to plug the cable back in. Any questions?" asked Eric.

"How long can I spend in the playroom?" Lina asked.

"Good question! You can disconnect for about 20 minutes once in the morning and once in the afternoon," answered Eric.

"Ok, kiddo, time to go," Jake said to Sam. "You're coming back tomorrow for a movie in the afternoon as long as Lina feels up to it!"

"Okaaaaaay," Sam and Lina fist-bumped each other. "See you tomorrow, Lina!"

"Thanks, Sam," Lina said.

After dinner, Lina and her mom got into their pajamas and brushed their teeth. Lina's mom asked, "Want to read a book?"

Lina yawned, "Great." Lina fell asleep before she finished the second page.

Liz set up her chair bed and fell asleep almost immediately when her head hit the pillow. A couple of hours later, Lina yelled out, "Mom!"

Liz sat up with a start. "What's wrong, honey?"

"Oh. I forgot where I was - it's weird waking up to a strange place, this monitor is so bright and I hear someone crying. Why are people up in the middle of the night?" Lina asked.

"Well, it's a hospital and things happen all night," her mom replied. "Can you get into bed with me?" Lina pleaded.

Jeannine walked in the room, "Is everything okay in here?"

"Lina woke up and I just pressed the button on the EEG recorder," said Liz, "She wants me to sleep with her. Is that okay?"

"Sure," said Jeannine, "Whatever makes Lina comfortable."

Liz and Lina arranged themselves in Lina's hospital bed and soon fell asleep.

12

Call Button

"**What should we** do today?" Lina asked.

"Well, we have some visitors coming later this morning, but we have a couple of hours. I suppose we should do what we usually do—go to the bathroom, get dressed, brush our teeth, wash our faces and eat something. Then we can check out these bags and do something fun."

"Sounds good to me!" said Lina.

They dove into the bags of crafts with wild abandon. Lina made a collage, painted a canvas, and did some coloring. Her mom joined in and took some pictures for their school presentation.

In the middle of the morning, Lina and Mom went to the playroom.

The volunteers were doing face painting. Lina got a heart on her cheek. Twenty minutes flew by and they picked out some videos for later.

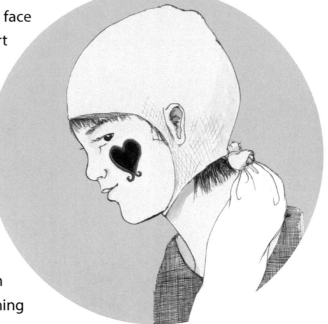

The afternoon was full of visitors and then Sam came back after dinner for a movie date. "Hey, what's up?" asked Sam, as she came in the door with Mary, "Anything to report?"

"It's not what I thought it was going to be,   Sam!" said Lina. "It's not scary or boring. I mean I wish I could be outside playing, but it's not that bad. Mom and I picked out a couple of movies from the playroom. What do you want to watch?" Lina said.

"Let me check out the selection." Sam held up one of the DVDs.

"Oooh! I love this one about the girl who starts her own cookie company!"

Liz popped it into the DVD player and she and Mary headed out the door, "We are going to be right across the hall getting some snacks from the family pantry."

The girls were snuggled on the bed when the moms returned and everyone settled in to watch the movie. The lead character had just sold her first box of cookies when Lina turned to Sam and opened her mouth to speak but nothing came out. She fell back on the bed shaking.

Liz reached over and hit the nurse call button. Nurses were already coming into the room. Sam jumped off the bed and ran to her mom. Soon Lina stopped shaking. Lina's eyes were open and the nurses were showing her pictures and asking her questions.

"What is your name?" Lina didn't respond.

"Where are you?" Lina said nothing.

"Point to the ceiling." Lina didn't point.

"Point to the window." Lina didn't move.

"What is this?" A nurse asked, showing her a picture of scissors. When Lina didn't say anything, the nurse said, "This is a pair of scissors. Remember I showed you the scissors."

The nurse did this two more times with a picture of an apple and a dog.

Lina blinked a couple of times and tried to sit up. Liz reached out for Lina's hand. "Honey, I'm right here."

"I'm… I'm…" Lina tried to speak.

"It's okay. Just breathe and relax. Everyone is here is take care of you," a nurse said.

Liz continued to hold Lina's hand and a nurse helped her sit up in bed. He repeated the questions he had asked before. This time Lina could answer, giving her name, where she was, and pointing to the ceiling and window. Then he asked her if she remembered the pictures he showed her. She didn't.

"Does that mean something is wrong with my brain?" Asked Lina.

He replied, "This is a test to see if you are aware during the seizure. I'll give the doctor the information and it can help us, along with the video and the EEG to see where the seizure might have been coming from in your brain. Drink some water and try to get some rest."

Lina turned to her mom, "Can Sam stay with me tonight?"

"Can I? Please, mom?" Sam turned to her mom.

"I'm so sorry, kiddo. You can't. It's the rules." Sam looked disappointed.

"This is so unfair! Why can't I stay with my friend? She is going through all of this," Sam gestured around the room with her hands flying, "and I'm supposed to help her but I can't even do that."

"It's okay, Sam," Lina started to say, but Sam cut her off.

"No. It's. Not." Sam declared, "I'm so sorry I have to leave. I feel like I'm not being a good friend at all."

Sam hung her head sorrowfully and Mary put her arm around her, "Let's say goodbye, honey. We can come back in the morning."

Sam walked over to Lina's bed, "I'm sorry I can't stay but I'll come back tomorrow. Pinky promise." The girls latched pinkies and shook.

As they left, Sam heard Lina ask her mom to sleep with her again.

Liz answered, "Of course I can."

MY SEIZURE CALENDAR

EPILEPSY FOUNDATION
END EPILEPSY TOGETHER

Seizure Calendar for: _____ Dates: _____ to _____ Year _____

Seizure Key: Describe type of seizures and label by using one of the letters below. Use one letter for each different type of seizure. Record the number of seizures using the seizure key on the dates they occur. Females can note the day of their menstrual cycle next to 'cycle' day. Note if any triggers such as missed or changes in medicines, changes in sleep, diet, or activity, stress, or other illness.

Type A: _____   Type C: _____

Type B: _____   Type D: _____

SUNDAY	MONDAY	TUESDAY	WEDNESDAY	THURSDAY	FRIDAY	SATURDAY
Date: _____ Cycle: _____ Event:	Date: _____ Cycle: _____ Event:	Date: _____ Cycle: _____ Event:	Date: _____ Cycle: _____ Event:	Date: _____ Cycle: _____ Event:	Date: _____ Cycle: _____ Event:	Date: _____ Cycle: _____ Event:
Date: _____ Cycle: _____ Event:	Date: _____ Cycle: _____ Event:	Date: _____ Cycle: _____ Event:	Date: _____ Cycle: _____ Event:	Date: _____ Cycle: _____ Event:	Date: _____ Cycle: _____ Event:	Date: _____ Cycle: _____ Event:
Date: _____ Cycle: _____ Event:	Date: _____ Cycle: _____ Event:	Date: _____ Cycle: _____ Event:	Date: _____ Cycle: _____ Event:	Date: _____ Cycle: _____ Event:	Date: _____ Cycle: _____ Event:	Date: _____ Cycle: _____ Event:
Date: _____ Cycle: _____ Event:	Date: _____ Cycle: _____ Event:	Date: _____ Cycle: _____ Event:	Date: _____ Cycle: _____ Event:	Date: _____ Cycle: _____ Event:	Date: _____ Cycle: _____ Event:	Date: _____ Cycle: _____ Event:
Date: _____ Cycle: _____ Event:	Date: _____ Cycle: _____ Event:	Date: _____ Cycle: _____ Event:	Date: _____ Cycle: _____ Event:	Date: _____ Cycle: _____ Event:	Date: _____ Cycle: _____ Event:	Date: _____ Cycle: _____ Event:

Used with permission from the Epilepsy Foundation of America, Inc., © 2020.

13

A Mystery

Lina slept through the night and in the morning she woke up to the sun shining through the windows. Dr. Maleni came into Lina's room.

Lina said, "I had a seizure last night—or we think it was."

"It was a seizure, Lina. I printed it out for you to see what was going on." Dr. Maleni pointed to Lina's head. "It's this area right here and we know now that your medication was working to control your seizures, but we need to increase it now and add another medication."

Liz said, "Will you do that today? And will we see a difference right away?"

"We are going to keep you another night," Dr. Maleni said. "We want to see if there are any changes. Based on this EEG, we can make an official diagnosis of epilepsy."

"Oh, so I guess the great mystery is solved," Lina said sadly.

"Actually, no, Lina. The big mystery is not solved." Dr. Maleni crouched low to look directly in Lina's eyes, "Every patient I have deals with the mystery of epilepsy. Sometimes medications work and sometimes they don't. EEGs are valuable to give us evidence over and over when someone has seizures."

"So, even though I have epilepsy, I still have more adventures and mysteries to solve?" Lina asked.

"Yes—and with your attitude of being curious, making connections from the evidence we gather, and working with us as a team, we can get closer to solving each mystery as it comes up," responded Dr. Maleni with a smile.

"Oh, okay, so I guess this detective is still on the case," Lina said with a sigh. "This is not how I thought this was going to go down. I guess I thought every answer brings us closer to solving the mystery."

"I know, Lina." Liz put her arm around her and held her close.

Sunday felt a little longer than before. Lina wanted to be done with the test and go back to school. Her mom tried to keep her occupied with more crafts and movies, but it was the visit from framily that cheered her up the most.

Mary and Sam came to visit on Sunday afternoon. "How are you, Lina?" Mary asked. Lina tried to smile but it came out as a grimace, "Okay."

"What's up?" Asked Sam.

"I have epilepsy, but it's still a mystery—will the meds work? I don't know! After the other seizure yesterday, Dr. Maleni says I have to stay and I don't want to stay, I just want to go to school and it's sort of annoying but everyone is being so nice I kinda feel like I can't be upset about it." The words came out in a rush and tears rolled down Lina's face. "Even you got upset yesterday. This is so hard."

Sam grabbed Lina's hand, "I'm sorry. It's okay to be sad. I would be sad. You are being so cool about it so much of the time. Like how you and I taught everyone at school. You are kicking epilepsy's butt. And sorry I got upset yesterday. It's hard to see you, you know, have a seizure."

Liz moved in and wiped tears from her own eyes, "Honey, we have all been treating this as a great adventure, but it's scary and frustrating, too."

"Mom, look, I just made you cry," Lina moaned, "That's not cool."

"Lina, let me tell you something," her mom started. "This is not the first time I have cried and it won't be the last. You are my daughter and all of the stuff happening to you makes me worry for you because I love you so much. Those are the facts. But we are not going to drown in tears. We are so lucky to have great doctors and help. We are going to cry together, laugh together and live as normally as possible. We are in this as a family."

"And as a framily?" Lina asked.

"Yup," said Sam.

"Yes," agreed Mary, "As framily. Why do you think we are here?"

Sam suddenly remembered. "And we brought food—which is getting cold! Feeling good enough to eat?"

Lina and Liz hugged and wiped their tears, "Definitely," said Lina. "Crying always makes me hungry."

Before Lina and Liz went to bed, they did a video chat with Jake and Nate. Even though they wanted to visit, Nate had an ear infection so Jake decided to keep him home and stay with him.

"Ina! Ina! Ina! Ove oo!" Nate yelled into the camera. Their conversation was fun but short because Nate kept hanging up on them.

Lina and Liz woke up the next day and did their usual routine. After a breakfast of pancakes and fruit, Dr. Maleni came into the room.

"I have some good news," Dr. Maleni said, "Your EEG over the last 24 hours since you had the seizure has been showing only spikes. The medicine is controlling the seizure activity. So you'll be going home today. The tech will be in here later this morning. Definitely order lunch as I expect you'll leave around two o'clock."

"Thank you so much, Dr. Maleni! Yay!" Lina exclaimed.

"Can I have a hug and a selfie, doctor? It's for my presentation at school...the selfie, not the hug," said Lina.

Dr. Maleni laughed, "Yes to both!"

About a half hour later, there was a knock on the door. Sam was standing there with flowers and Mary had coffee for Liz.

"Awwwww," Lina said, "That's so cool! Guess what? The doctor said

I could go home. What are you guys doing here?"

"I texted them on the sly when the doctor said you could go home," Liz said.

While Liz and Mary sipped their coffee and chatted, the girls sat on the bed. Lina reached over and put the checkerboard on the bed. "Ready for a rematch?" asked Lina.

"Wow! I don't remember the last time we played a checkers..." Sam's voice trailed off and she realized it was when Lina had her first seizure.

"I remember, and you do too. I can see it," Lina said slowly, putting her hand on Sam's arm. "And it's okay. You don't have to be careful what you say. We are always going to remember that moment. And even though I have epilepsy, I'm so glad that we went through this adventure together. Thank you for being my friend and framily."

The girls hugged.

Gifts for You, the Reader

Thank you for reading *Lina's EEG Adventure*. It is our hope that you found the book helpful and it provided you with some insight into the journey from seizure to diagnosis.

Our goal with this book is to help as many children and families affected by epilepsy as possible. By sharing the testing experience and sharing different ways friends and families can be helpful during this challenging time, we hope to destigmatize this disease and create more empathy. Knowledge is power.

Please go to our website *www.linaseegadventure.com/bonus* to get one or more bonus gifts:

* Reading guide for book clubs
* Coloring pages of Lina and Sam
* A PDF guide to helping your child or friend through medical tests.

Thank you!

Resources

The following resources are among the many excellent sources of information available to people and families whose lives are affected by epilepsy.

Epilepsy Foundation—Provides national and community resources to support people, friends and families affected by epilepsy. There is a 24/7 helpline, resources, and connections to specialists.
https://www.epilepsy.com

Epilepsy Foundation Kids' Crew—This branch of the Epilepsy Foundation is run by kids and a place where young people (14 and younger) who have epilepsy, are a support person to someone with epilepsy or want to educate others about epilepsy can get resources and information. There are opportunities to learn, volunteer, and take part in challenges and virtual events.
https://www.epilepsy.com/make-difference/get-involved/kids-crew

American Epilepsy Society—The website contains clinical resources, patient support resources, research, news, and more links to local organizations and jobs in the field.
https://www.aesnet.org/

CURE (Citizens United for Research in Epilepsy)—A site with a wealth of knowledge from research, news, patient support to a podcast covering topics and people's intimate experiences. There is a fundraising component that supports research.
https://www.cureepilepsy.org/

Glossary

Seizure—A seizure happens when there is unusual activity in someone's brain. It can affect the way a person acts or a appears for a short amount of time.

Neurologist—A specialist doctor who studies and understands the functions of the brain.

EEG—Short for electroencephalogram. Electrodes are attached to wires and placed in specific places around a person's head. The wires are connected to a computer that records electrical activity in a person's brain. An EEG can be done in an office or hospital. It can also be ambulatory, meaning that it is carried around with the person in a backpack or bag the person carries.

Spikes—On an EEG reading, the spikes are an indication of abnormal brain activity; sometimes they indicate the start of a seizure.

Seizure Action Plans can help you organize your seizure information and have it available when and where you need it. A prepared plan can help you know what to do to prevent an emergency or tell others what to do in emergency situations. You can also adapt these plans to different situations in your life.

SEIZURE ACTION PLAN (SAP)

Name: _____ Birth Date: _____

Address: _____ Phone: _____

Parent/Guardian: _____ Phone: _____

Emergency Contact/Relationship _____ Phone: _____

Seizure Information

Seizure Type	How Long It Lasts	How Often	What Happens

Protocol for seizure during school (check all that apply) ☑

- ☐ First aid – **Stay. Safe. Side.**
- ☐ Give rescue therapy according to SAP
- ☐ Notify parent/emergency contact
- ☐ Contact school nurse at _____
- ☐ Call 911 for transport to _____
- ☐ Other _____

✚ First aid for any seizure

- ○ **STAY** calm, keep calm, **begin timing seizure**
- ○ Keep me **SAFE** – remove harmful objects, don't restrain, protect head
- ○ **SIDE** – turn on side if not awake, keep airway clear, don't put objects in mouth
- ○ **STAY** until recovered from seizure
- ○ Swipe magnet for VNS
- ○ Write down what happens _____
- ○ Other _____

When to call 911

- ○ Seizure (loss of consciousness) longer than 5 minutes
- ○ Repeated seizures without recovery between them
- ○ Rescue medicine/therapy doesn't work
- ○ Injury occurs or suspected, seizure in water
- ○ Difficulty breathing after seizure
- ○ Person does not return to usual behavior after seizure
- ○ First time seizure
- ○ Other medical problems or pregnancy need to be checked

▣ When **rescue therapy** may be needed:

WHEN AND WHAT TO DO

If seizure (cluster, # or length) _____

Name of Med/Rx _____ How much to give (dose) _____

How to give _____

If seizure (cluster, # or length) _____

Name of Med/Rx _____ How much to give (dose) _____

How to give _____

If seizure (cluster, # or length) _____

Name of Med/Rx _____ How much to give (dose) _____

How to give _____

By helping you be prepared, seizures or the fear of seizures won't prevent you from participating and enjoying your life to the fullest. Here is a sample of a Seizure Action Plan that can be used in school. This and many other helpful forms can be downloaded from ww.epilepsy.com.

Seizure Action Plan *continued*

Care after seizure

What type of help is needed? (describe): _____

_____

When is student able to resume usual activity? _____

Special instructions

First Responders: _____

_____

Emergency Department: _____

_____

Daily seizure medicine

Medicine Name	Total Daily Amount	Amount of Tab/Liquid	How Taken (time of each dose and how much)

Other information

Triggers: _____

Important Medical History _____

Allergies _____

Epilepsy Surgery (type, date, side effects) _____

Device: ☐ VNS ☐ RNS ☐ DBS Date Implanted _____

Diet Therapy ☐ Ketogenic ☐ Low Glycemic ☐ Modified Atkins ☐ Other (describe) _____

Special Instructions: _____

_____

Health care contacts

Epilepsy Provider: _____ Phone: _____

Primary Care: _____ Phone: _____

Preferred Hospital: _____ Phone: _____

Pharmacy: _____ Phone: _____

My signature _____ Date _____

Provider signature _____ Date _____

Epilepsy.com

©2020 Epilepsy Foundation of America, Inc.
Revised 01/2020   130SRP/PAB1216

Provided Courtesy of

EPILEPSY FOUNDATION
END EPILEPSY TOGETHER

About the Creators

Photo by Sherry Sutton

Danielle Perrotta is a passionate educator and enjoys teaching children with diverse learning styles and challenges to be successful academically and creatively. As a special-needs mom of a daughter with epilepsy, she was inspired to write a book to share the journey from seizure to diagnosis. Danielle lives in Maplewood, NJ with her two children and loves to play the ukulele, go for walks in the South Mountain Reservation and shop local.

Tracy J. Nishimoto was born and raised in Hawai'i. She has had a varied career, teaching English to Japanese middle schoolers, designing theatrical costumes and working in film. She lives in Seattle. This is her first book.

Acknowledgments

This book would not have been possible without my own journey as a mom with a child affected by epilepsy. I want to thank my daughter, Bella, for her positivity, tenacity, and loving nature. Lina's experience is based on our story. Thank you to my son, Caleb, who makes us laugh, is optimistic and resilient in every sense of the word. Thank you to my parents, Carol and Dan Perrotta, who taught me to learn, be a researcher and a problem-solver and who show us much love and care. My grandparents, Mary Rose and Tony Perrotta, believed in me beyond all measure and started telling me to write at age 5 when I came up with stories—the memories of their encouragement lift me up. Special thanks to my brother, Anthony, and my Aunt, Rosanna, who were supportive from seizure to diagnosis and ready to take my teary phone calls with words that uplifted and made me smile.

I thank all my family for their support, love and encouragement during our journey and the creation of this book.

Thank you, thank you, thank you to my publisher, Thomas West, who imagined that my little slide show could be a chapter book. Thank you, Tom, for your belief, unending patience, and taking this book beyond where I could ever dream.

Tracy J. Nishimoto, what a dream come true to have you as an artist on this book. Your beautiful drawings bring the words and emotions on the page to life—I am so lucky to know you and appreciate all of the beauty and specificity in each illustration.

Special thanks to Jennifer Wallace Grady, Jonathan Nielsen and Tim Casart for providing their design expertise at the start of this project. Your input and support helped us along the way.

Sherry Sutton, my gratitude for your friendship goes beyond what can be written on this page. We have been friends since our children were in our bellies during yoga class. You have journeyed far and wide with me through the ups and downs of parenthood, life and I am so lucky to call you my Spiritual Sister. Your generosity in bringing this book to life through the marketing, logo, and your encouraging push towards the light has been amazing.

Dennis Mosner, thank you for taking beautiful pictures of our family to be used for the basis of the technical aspects of the book and to inspire and commemorate our EEG experience.

Thank you to the West family, who all had a hand in helping bring this book to life. You are incredibly inspiring to me, Miranda, and your enthusiasm, joy and determination is an asset to you, your family, and everyone you meet. I am so inspired by your advocacy and role in the world—the world is lucky to have you as an activist, leader, and friend. I can't wait to see where your journeys take you!

Thank you to the team of neurologists and epileptologists at the Institute of Neurology at St. Barnabas Hospital. Special thanks to Dr. Rajeshwari Mahalingham,

Dr. Eric B. Geller, and Dr. Orrin Devinsky. There are numerous ways that you have supported us by showing care, humanity and empathy, providing encouragement, and sharing your research. You have made a positive impact on this book and on our lives. I come away much more educated from each office visit and from lectures at FACES events.

Oh friends, thank you for your love—I am so lucky to have more framily that I can name here. Thank you Jacqueline Helgren, Kristin Suess, Grace Berman, Todd Lortie, Alissa Gardenhire, Meredith Hemphill, Melanie Kidd, Cris Valencia, Nicole Pivnick, Mark Goldberg, Devon Summersgill, Paul Holtzman and so many more. And to the Maplewood community FB group, MM, and families and friends all over the SOMA community, I am blessed to be living here and to get feedback and support from you and your kids.

To the staff at Link Community Charter School, I am grateful to be in the world of education and supporting our scholars alongside amazing colleagues.

I have such gratitude to the people who read my book, gave me feedback, provided editing, and suggested questions for the book club discussions. The universe blessed me with the gift to teach and to encourage—my students and families from over 18 years in teaching have infused my life with stories of hope, resilience, and courage. Thank you for being along on this journey.

—Danielle Perrotta

Amarna Books and Media would like to thank the Epilepsy Foundation for their assistance in providing us with the information graphics in the book as well as the use of "Stay, Safe, Side" in Chapter 9.

Made in the USA
Las Vegas, NV
15 December 2020

12681735R00062